'It might be better for the team's sake if I simply packed up being captain like Luke wants . . .' .

Everything is going wrong for Chris. His captaincy of the Danebridge school football team has got off to a terrible start, and no-one – least of all Chris himself – is sure he can do the job. And now, worst of all, Grandad is ill . . .

But then Chris has a brilliant idea. A challenge match against his brother Andrew and the other Danebridge Old Boys would give his team a chance to prove themselves once and for all. But Chris is taking a big risk . . .

ROB CHILDS is a Leicestershire teacher with many years experience of coaching and organizing school and area representative sports teams.

Also available by Rob Childs, and
published by Young Corgi Books:

THE BIG MATCH
THE BIG DAY
THE BIG HIT
THE BIG GOAL
THE BIG KICK
THE BIG GAME
THE BIG PRIZE
THE BIG CHANCE
THE BIG STAR


For older readers, published by Corgi
Yearling Books:

SOCCER AT SANDFORD
SANDFORD ON TOUR

# THE BIG KICK

## ROB CHILDS

### Illustrated by Tim Marwood

## YOUNG CORGI BOOKS

# THE BIG KICK
## A YOUNG CORGI BOOK  0  552  52663  0

First published in Great Britain

PRINTING HISTORY
Young Corgi edition published 1991
Reprinted 1991, 1992, 1993, 1994, 1995

This book is set in 14/18pt Century Schoolbook
by Kestrel Data, Exeter

Young Corgi Books are published by Transworld Publishers Ltd,
61–63 Uxbridge Road, Ealing, London W5 5SA,
in Australia by Transworld Publishers (Australia) Pty Ltd,
15–25 Helles Avenue, Moorebank, NSW 2170,
and in New Zealand by Transworld Publishers (NZ) Ltd,
3 William Pickering Drive, Albany, Auckland.

Printed and bound in Great Britain by
Cox & Wyman Ltd, Reading, Berkshire

In memory of Shane

# 1 Captain Chris

'Me? Captain! Why me?'

'Because, Christopher, I happen to think you're the right lad for the job,' Mr Jones smiled.

Chris Weston wasn't at all sure about that. He had simply been looking forward to playing in goal for Danebridge Primary School in the new soccer season. The last thing he had expected was to be captain.

'But what about Luke Bradshaw and the others?' Chris asked, still

stunned. 'Most of them are a year older than me.'

'Age doesn't come into it,' the headmaster said. 'I want a captain who can be trusted to set a proper example to his players on and off the field – somebody like you.'

Chris was thrilled but he feared

that his surprise selection might not go down too well at first, especially with Luke. And he was right.

'A goalie's no good as captain,' Luke claimed loudly to a group of the footballers later that same day. 'It should be the best player out on the pitch.'

'And who's that then?' Rakesh Patel put in cheekily.

'Me, of course!' Luke boasted. 'Who else? I'm gonna be our top scorer this season.'

'So? That doesn't prove anything,' Rakesh argued.

'Just watch it, Patel!' Luke warned, putting his fist under Rakesh's nose. 'Anybody here will tell you I'm the best. Right, you lot?'

It was more of a threat than a request for support. Luke glared

round at them fiercely and they did their duty by nodding.

'And I should have been captain. Right?' Again the nods. 'Right! That Weston's got it comin' to him now for this. You wait. Stupid old Jonesy's gone and made a big mistake pickin' *him*.'

As Chris lay slumped on the hard ground of the goalmouth, well beaten for the fifth time in the match, he might easily have been tempted to agree.

The season had already begun badly with two defeats in a row and now they were heading for their third. And to make matters worse, he realized that Luke Bradshaw had come to stand over him and gloat.

'Oh, yeah, brilliant captain you are,' Luke sneered. 'What yer goin' to do about this mess?'

Chris hauled himself heavily to his feet. Despite their age difference, he was nearly as tall as Luke and could look him straight in the face. 'It might help if you came back to do your share of the work in defence for a change,' he grumbled.

'I'm a striker,' Luke spat out. 'I'm here to score goals, not stop 'em.'

'So why don't you go off and score a few for us then?'

'Huh! I would do if you wallies ever got the ball over the halfway line to me.'

'That's not fair,' Chris said, fed up with Luke's constant taunting during the past fortnight. 'We're out-numbered every time they attack.'

Luke shrugged. 'That's your problem, Weston, not mine. You're the one who's supposed to be captain. Now if Jonesy had chose me in the first place . . .'

He left the rest unsaid as Mr Jones, the referee, trotted towards them. 'The game's not over yet,' he urged. 'Keep shouting your teammates on, Chris. Don't let them give up.'

Left alone as Luke went to kick off again, Chris grunted to himself. 'Team*mates*, he calls them! I won't have any mates left soon, if Bradshaw has his way.'

A voice close behind made him jump. 'Cheer up, little brother. Not

your fault. You had no chance with that shot.'

Chris swivelled round to see Andrew leaning on the goalpost, smirking. 'How long have you been there?'

'Just arrived. Grandad picked me up from school in the car,' Andrew said. 'Never knew he could drive so fast in that old banger of his. I guess he wanted to get back to watch you play as much as I did.'

Chris looked across to the touchline and spotted Grandad refilling his pipe. 'I wondered where he was. He's missed most of the game now, thanks to you being too lazy to catch the bus.'

'Hasn't missed much by the sound of it. 5–0, is it?'

'5–1 actually, if you must know. Rakesh scored.'

Andrew laughed. 'Danebridge are useless this year without all the old superstars like me. That guy was given a free shot at goal there. Now if I'd still been playing, he wouldn't have smelt it . . .'

'Belt up, will you!' Chris hissed. 'You're putting me off. I don't want to let any more in.'

He very nearly did straightaway. A centre from the left was only partly cleared and he was forced to make two good saves, one after the other. Chris booted the ball a long way upfield to relieve his frustrations, half-wishing he could do the same to Luke's head.

'Well stopped, our kid!' Andrew praised him, ignoring his younger brother's bad mood. 'You show 'em you mean to make a fight of it.'

15

Chris pulled a face. He knew the real fight he had on his hands was more how to cope with Luke Bradshaw's spoiling everything by his efforts to bully the team into turning against their own captain.

His goal was peppered with shots right up till the final whistle and nobody was more pleased to hear it blow than Chris. When he started to give their opponents three cheers, however, he wasn't surprised to get only a weak response and he slunk sadly over to the touchline.

'Oh, dear,' Grandad said, seeing the boy's face. 'Don't take it to heart, Chris. You tried your best.'

'Not good enough, though, was it? I mean, I can't go charging around all over the pitch sorting things out like other captains can.'

'Your team really would be in trouble if their goalie went berserk like that!' Grandad chuckled. 'Anyway, it's not necessary. You get on and do it your own way.'

'I wish I could, but . . .' Chris checked himself before blurting out anything to Grandad about Luke, '. . . but it's just not the same without Andrew and the rest we had last season.'

'You shouldn't say that. They're all in the past now. Give it time. You'll see. I'm sure things will work out fine in the end.'

'I hope you're right, Grandad, but how long's that going to take?'

As Chris trailed off to the wooden changing hut, Grandad stroked his

moustache thoughtfully and sighed. 'I don't know, kids these days. Problems, problems . . .'

He wandered across to his stone cottage which stood at the side of the village recreation ground and paused at the back gate for a few minutes to finish smoking his pipe. All of a sudden he winced and rubbed his hand gently over his chest, puzzled at the painful twinge he'd just felt.

'Ooh, spot of indigestion, I bet, all this rushing about,' he wheezed, tucking his still-warm pipe into his jacket pocket. 'Reckon it's time to go and put my feet up with a cup of tea.'

# 2  Help!

'Uugh!'

Chris's breath was knocked out of him in a loud grunt as he dived down at Rakesh's feet in the scramble around his goal. But he came up grinning and triumphant with the ball safely hugged to his chest.

'Great stuff, little brother,' Andrew called. 'To me now.'

Chris hurled the ball away and sucked in another deep breath. 'Phew! Just what I needed this, a good hard

workout on the recky with all the old
gang.'

'All right for you maybe,' Rakesh
muttered. 'I could have scored.'

Chris laughed. 'Can't let you do that
or I'd never shut you up! Now clear off
and stop goal-hanging.'

Rakesh Patel was one of the few
members of the present primary
school team allowed to join in the
rough and tumble game the following
Saturday afternoon. Mostly it was
boys of Andrew's age, now at Selworth
Comprehensive, glad to be free of
homework at the weekend and
wanting to run off some surplus
energy.

Rakesh loped away but was soon
back again, jinking down the wing
with the ball before curling over a high

cross. Tim Lawrence, last season's Danebridge captain, met it with a header just wide of Chris's lunging hands.

'Goal!' Tim cried in delight.

'Rubbish!' Andrew retorted. 'Post. Would have hit the post and gone wide.'

Since their posts were only a jumbled collection of coats, there was the usual lively argument as to whether or not the goal would count.

'C'mon, let's give it to them, Andrew,' Chris said after fetching the ball from the hedge. 'We're still winning.'

Andrew's face clouded for a moment then lightened again. 'Aw, all right, suppose so,' he grinned. 'We'll be generous – that's 5–2 to us.'

'4–2, you mean,' Tim corrected him quickly. 'That shot of yours was over the bar.'

'What bar? It was well in.'

'You must want your eyes tested,' Tim said, shoving him playfully.

Chris smiled to himself. 'Just like old times,' he thought as he hoofed the ball back into play to get everyone moving again.

He glanced across to where a black and white border collie was snuffling around at the bottom of Grandad's garden wall. 'Keep an eye on Shoot, please, Grandad,' Chris called out. 'We don't want him coming on the pitch.'

Grandad was supposed to be looking after their dog while they were playing, but he seemed more interested in watching the action than in checking what Shoot was up to. Pipe drooping from his mouth, Grandad made no effort to reply, and Chris was forced to turn his mind back on the game as Tim fed the ball cleverly through for John Duggan.

With people like the bruising Duggie on the loose, Chris had to have all his wits about him. Sprinting from his goal, he just won the race for the ball, pushing it to safety as they collided solidly and sprawled together on the grass.

The attacker's quick temper might once have easily flared up at being blocked like that by the young keeper, but Chris had gradually earned his respect. 'Next time, little Westy, I'll get you back, you'll see,' Duggie

grinned, helping Chris to his feet.

'Don't bet on it,' Chris said, rubbing his arm, but when the next time did come, neither was given a chance to prove their point.

With Chris out of position after making another save, Duggie was about to slot the ball into the unguarded goal when, to his fury, it was suddenly whipped off his toes by an excited pitch invader.

'Shoot!' cried Chris.

'I was just going to!' Duggie yelled angrily. 'He robbed me.'

'I didn't mean that,' Chris shouted, equally upset. 'Come here, Shoot. Leave it!'

But as the players began to chase around after him, Shoot kept on

bopping the ball along with his head, barking madly.

'Hey! Stupid hound, get out of it,' Duggie screamed. 'You stopped me scoring.'

'Can't you control your dog?' Tim demanded of Andrew. 'He's wrecking the game.'

'Shoot! Come, Shoot!' chorused both Andrew and Chris, but this only confused the animal even more as he scuttled from one to the other, jumping up at them.'

'Send him off!' Rakesh chuckled. 'Show him the red card.'

'Down, boy,' said Andrew crossly. 'What's got into you?'

'Where's Grandad?' Chris piped up, noticing his absence from the wall for the first time. 'I didn't see him go in.'

'Well he has, and he's let Shoot scarper,' Tim complained. 'Put him on the lead, will you, so we can get on with our soccer.'

The collie's yelping was growing ever more desperate as he began to dash backwards and forwards between the cottage and the pitch. Every time one of the boys bent to grab his collar, he would twist about to shoot away again.

It was Rakesh who was the first to realize. 'Hey, I think he's trying to tell you something, Chris. The way he's behaving, perhaps he wants you to follow him.'

Chris's anger towards his disobedient dog vanished immediately and he felt his stomach churn over. A terrible thought suddenly hit him like

a cold sponge. 'Grandad! Where *is* he?'

When Chris began to run towards the cottage, wildly waving Andrew to join him, the game was abandoned and the other players either stood around or wandered after them out of curiosity.

Chris hurtled through the gate and his legs almost buckled beneath him at what he saw. Grandad had collapsed and was lying flat out on the ground behind the wall, his hands over his chest and his face screwed up in pain.

'Grandad! What's the matter?' he cried, tears welling up as Shoot crouched by Grandad's head to lick his ear. 'Can you speak?'

To Chris's utter relief, Grandad slowly opened his eyes. 'Sorry, m'boy,'

he groaned. 'Came over a bit dizzy, like. Must have fainted.'

'Andrew!' Chris exclaimed as his brother knelt down beside him, white-faced, and started to loosen Grandad's tie. 'I'll see to that. You get inside quick and dial 999!'

# 3 Down in the Dumps

Light from a street lamp leaked through the brothers' bedroom curtains and settled on two sorrowful faces staring up at the shadowy ceiling.

'Grandad *will* get better, won't he?' Chris whispered from his bed.

'Course he will,' Andrew insisted, finding comfort himself in his own words. 'You heard the doctor. She said Grandad just needed to rest up a bit and take things easy for a while.'

They fell silent again, remembering how much Grandad had helped them in so many ways, especially in their sports. He'd given each of them a ball to kick almost from the moment they were able to walk.

'Been overdoing it in his garden recently, I bet,' Andrew murmured. 'When he gets back home from hospital, we'll be round there all the time to see he's OK and got everything he needs, do his shopping and so on.'

'Right,' Chris agreed. 'We can even finish off that digging for him as well. And let him have Shoot for company every day.'

'Yeah, good old Shoot – what a hero!' cheered Andrew, sitting up on his

pillow. 'Lassie couldn't have saved Grandad any better.'

The memory of that awful moment when he had found Grandad slumped behind the wall made Chris shudder. 'I thought at first he was . . . well, you know . . .'

'I know,' Andrew said softly. 'It seemed to take yonks for that ambulance to arrive. Was I glad when Mum came and took over . . .'

He stopped. 'Hey, how did Mum know what had happened?'

'Rakesh fetched her. He ran all the way here – said it was quicker than phoning!' Chris explained, then added, 'He's a good pal, Rakesh. I wish I had a few more like him at school.'

'Why do you say that?'

Slowly, Chris at last began to tell

Andrew of all his troubles over the captaincy. He felt he could talk about such things at a time like this without the risk of being laughed at.

Chris need not have worried. Andrew was in fact so shocked that he climbed out of bed and went to perch on the edge of his brother's. 'You mean your own teammates are getting at you?'

'No, it's just Luke basically, I suppose,' Chris said. 'But he's making some of the others gang up on me a bit, taking the mickey and that. They're scared of him.'

'Well I'm not!' exclaimed Andrew. 'Want me – and Duggie – to go and sort Bradshaw out for you?'

'No!' Chris almost shouted, jolting upright. 'That would only make matters worse. I'll fight my own battles, thanks.'

Andrew grunted. 'Humph! Mind you, I did warn you, remember, when old Jonesy chose you. I said some lads wouldn't like it.'

'OK, OK, but please don't go saying anything to Mum – and especially not Grandad,' Chris begged. 'I don't want him fretting over me right now. Anyway, it might be better for the team's sake, if I simply packed up being captain like Luke wants.'

'Don't do that!' Andrew gasped. 'If you give in to him, he'll think you're a softie and keep on at you even more. You can't let him get away with it.'

'No, I guess you're right, I'll think of something,' Chris sighed. 'But let's forget about *him* at the moment. Grandad's far more important. I just wish I could at least come up with the one thing which would be bound to make him feel better again.'

'What's that?'

'For him to see Danebridge start winning – and that might even help to solve my little problems too.'

They both knew that would be easier said than done . . .

And so it proved.

Danebridge lost again in midweek, 3–1 away, with Chris's mind more on Grandad, due home the next day, than it was on the game. He would normally have prevented two of the goals without any trouble, one of which he let slip straight through his legs.

As they waited in the school minibus for Mr Jones afterwards, Luke tried to show Chris up in front of the whole team.

'You're a rubbish captain, Weston, and you're a rubbish goalie too. We ain't got no chance with you around.'

'Leave him, Luke,' Rakesh cut in, signalling Chris to keep out of it. 'You know his grandad's ill.'

'So what! Who cares? C'mon, the rest of you, let's take a vote. Hands up all those who don't want Weston in the team.'

His own hand shot up into the air, daring anybody else not to do the same. Paul Walker, one of the defenders, rather shakily raised his

arm but somehow found his voice too. 'Wait a minute, Luke. I don't think Westy should be dropped, he's a good keeper really, it's just that . . .'

As Paul's courage failed him, Rakesh spoke up again before others were forced to join in the vote. 'I reckon we'd be much better off Luke, in fact, without *you* in the side. You're so slow, you wreck all our attacks.'

'Oh yeah! So who was it scored our goal today, eh?' Luke sneered.

'My baby sister could have scored that one,' Rakesh scoffed. 'But who was it who got subbed later as well?'

'Only came off 'cos I got crocked in that tackle.'

Rakesh laughed. 'Doubt it. If you ask me, Jonesy's sussed out at last that you're bone idle and selfish. You never pass the ball.'

Luke Bradshaw was furious. 'Who's asking you, Patel? Just wait till we get out of this old crate – I'm gonna do you.'

Chris could stand it no longer. 'Shut up, both of you!' he demanded, his cheeks flushed. 'No wonder we're doing so badly when we're getting at each other all the time. We'll never improve unless we start working together properly like we did last year.'

'Huh! Listen to him, he hardly ever played last year,' Luke cackled. 'We had a good team then with Simon Garner in goal.'

'Doesn't matter, Tim's lot have gone now,' Chris went on, refusing to be put

off, 'and it's up to us to show we don't need them any more.'

'And how yer goin' to see we do that, wonderboy?'

'Well, er . . .' In his desperation, a wild idea suddenly flashed into Chris's head like an S.O.S. flare. 'I guess we'll just have to prove it by playing them in a match and beating them.'

'Beat Tim's team! Don't make me laugh. You and whose army?'

Chris had no time to reply, even if he'd known what to say, as Mr Jones chose that moment to pull open the driver's door.

'Right, all in?' the headmaster asked. 'Everybody happy?'

Judging by their faces, he wasn't at all surprised when no-one answered.

# 4  Or Else . . .

'Shoot! Come here, boy.'

Hearing his name, the collie lifted his busy nose out of the undergrowth at the edge of the recky and looked up.

'Come, Shoot!' Chris ordered. He followed it with a whistle which only made the dog cock his head on one side, as if to question the real need for such an interruption.

When Shoot then went and buried his head once more into the long grass, Chris stamped his way across to him.

'Bad dog. Come when I call, will you? I haven't got all day.'

It took the lead and a good yank to get Shoot to leave whatever fascinating smells he'd found. But Chris soon got tired of being pulled this way and that by his frisky dog and let him dive away once again on some other invisible trail. He looked around, bored, hoping to pick out somebody he knew before returning to Grandad's. He did – Luke Bradshaw.

'Oh, no,' Chris groaned, but it was too late to turn back. As Luke's grubby red tracksuit emerged from the shadows at the rear of the changing hut, Chris saw that he was not alone. Paul Walker came out behind him.

'What yer doin' snoopin' round here, Weston?' Luke challenged him.

'Just walking the dog. Anyway, what are you two up to that's such a big secret?'

'None of your business, *captain*, so push off!' Luke snarled, glancing over to where Shoot's hindquarters were sticking up out of a clump of weeds some distance away. 'Seems that mongrel o' yours got some sense at least. Like us, he don't want you with him neither.'

Chris let the taunt pass, determined not to show Luke he was at all bothered by it. 'What's going on, Paul?' he called out instead.

He saw Paul check nervously back at the hut before answering. 'Nothing, Westy, we're just messing around.'

Before either of them could stop him, Chris brushed by and peered

behind the hut, spotting the gap in the wooden planking. 'Have you two done that?'

'No, we just found it like that,' Paul said quickly.

'The village team will be really mad if they think their hut's been vandalized,' Chris said, inspecting the damage. 'They might even stop us using it for our school matches.'

'So what?' sneered Luke. 'It's too draughty anyway.'

'It is now,' said Chris. 'That hole's big enough for somebody to squeeze through, I reckon.'

Paul grabbed a few pieces of wood that were propped up against the boards. 'Look, they're all rotten. They were coming loose so we were just

going to put 'em back in place again properly.'

'Yeah, that's right. We're doin' 'em a good turn, mendin' it, like,' Luke sniggered. 'And when's Jonesy's little pet gonna do us all a good turn by tellin' him he don't want to be captain no more?'

'Why should I do that?' Chris said, trying to stay cool.

'Cos you're rubbish, that's why. And cos if you don't a few of us will grab you one day and bend one of your fingers back till it breaks. You won't even be able to play in goal then.'

Luke shoved Chris as he spoke, pressing him up against the hut. But Chris had no chance to defend himself. Both boys were suddenly startled by a low, threatening growl.

'Watch out!' Paul cried. 'His dog's here.'

Luke stepped back in alarm but Chris reacted even faster. 'No, Shoot! It's OK. Quiet!'

The growl subsided to a rumble in Shoot's throat, but his eyes never left Luke while Chris slipped the lead's noose back over the dog's head. 'OK, finish, good boy,' he said soothingly.

'C'mon, Luke, let's go,' said Paul. 'I've fixed the hole.'

Luke tore his gaze away from Shoot. 'Right, you heard what I said, Weston. Think about it. Otherwise, some time when you're by yourself . . . no Andrew, no Rakesh, no Grandad around – and no dog to protect you . . .'

Luke turned and walked casually away, trying to make it seem as if he wasn't in any hurry. Chris was left fuming and bent down to stroke Shoot's head to calm them both down.

'Good boy, you sure came back at the right time for once then.'

Later that Sunday afternoon, when Andrew was making a cup of tea for

Grandad in the kitchen, Shoot suddenly jumped up from the floor and deafened him with his barking at the back door.

'Whatever's the matter with him?' Grandad called from the living room where he was talking with Chris.

'He must have heard something outside,' Andrew shouted.

'Let him out, will you, or shut him up,' Chris yelled over the din.

Andrew was fed up waiting for the kettle to boil anyway and followed the dog into the garden. Just in time to see a figure disappear over the wall on to the recky.

'Hey, you!' Andrew cried. 'Come back here!'

There was no chance of that. Shoot was already barking his head off between the bars of the gate, and by the time Andrew reached the wall the intruder had made his escape through another garden.

Chris had also scuttled out of the cottage to join them. 'Who was it? Did you see anything?'

'Just some kid in a red top. Come scrumping Grandad's apples, I bet,' Andrew laughed. 'He was lucky Shoot didn't jump over the wall and get hold of him.'

Chris grunted. 'I wish he had, if it was a red trackie you saw.'

'I'm seeing red too,' came an angry voice behind them. Neither had heard Grandad hobble down the lawn on his new walking stick, and they twirled round to stare at where he was now pointing it.

Graffiti had been sprayed right across the side of Grandad's garden shed in large, careless capital letters, the can of red paint lying abandoned on the ground in the panicky exit.

'The spelling's not much good,' said Andrew. 'Even mine's better than that.'

'It's not funny, Andrew,' Chris grimaced. 'I know somebody else who can't spell.'

'Why on earth should anybody want to write that on my shed?' demanded Grandad and read the warning out aloud. *'PACK UP OR ELSE* . . . What's that supposed to mean?'

Chris's face drained of colour. He didn't need three guesses to answer that one.

# 5 Challenge

Grandad's rocking chair creaked gently backwards and forwards as he sat listening to Chris explain about Luke and the hut.

'I wish you'd told me before what's been going on,' Grandad said. 'It's no good just bottling this kind of thing up inside.'

Out of habit, he reached into his pocket for his curved pipe and clamped it firmly in the corner of his mouth, much to Andrew's dismay.

'I thought the doctor told you to give up smoking, Grandad, after what happened. That's no good for you either.'

'Aye, you're quite right, m'boy. Pity! I rather enjoyed puffing on my old pipe when I had some thinking to do,' Grandad sighed. Then, with a twinkle in his eye, he added, 'But the doc said nowt about me not sucking it, did she?'

The brothers smiled and let Grandad suck away at his unlit pipe for a few minutes in peace until he seemed to reach a decision.

'Your headmaster was kind enough to come and visit me the other day, Chris,' he began, laying down the pipe. 'And he mentioned that some of the village team have had a bit of money stolen during recent matches.'

Chris turned even paler. 'From the changing hut?'

'Aye, you've guessed it,' Grandad replied. 'I shall have to report all this, I'm afraid. Fetch me the phone book, please.'

'Who are you going to ring?' asked Chris fearfully. 'The police?'

Grandad shook his head. 'Mr Jones – if he's at home. I may be wrong about the thefts, but I'm not going to have some little hooligan nip into my garden and start repainting my shed.'

He raised his hand to silence Chris's protests. 'I'm sorry, but it has to be done. We'll let the headmaster handle this now . . .'

Mr Jones was indeed swift to act.

'There's no place in any team of mine for a thief and a bully,' he told Luke Bradshaw in his office the next morning. 'You are banned from taking part in any further school sport here at Danebridge.'

The boy had refused to own up until Paul confessed to the headmaster how Luke had forced him to help make the hole at the back of the hut.

'He made me keep watch as well while he broke in,' Paul whimpered.

'He said he'd kill me if I blabbed.'

Paul was let off lightly after Chris had also spoken up for him, but it was too late for Luke to be forgiven.

'How right I was not to make you soccer captain this season!' Mr Jones sighed. 'I decided you didn't deserve the honour because of your bad behaviour in the past and now you've disgraced yourself completely.'

Luke attempted a shrug but somehow it didn't really come off. At lunchtime, after the news of his punishment had spread, he still tried to act tough, but the footballers sensed that the swagger had gone.

'You'll be lost without me,' he predicted spitefully.

'We were losing *with* you,' Rakesh mocked him. 'At least now we can start to enjoy our soccer again and show everybody how good a team we can really be, given a chance.'

Danebridge certainly didn't seem to miss Luke in their next game, avoiding defeat for the first time by drawing 1–1. Their better team spirit was obvious, with all the players willing to run their hearts out for one another. They were inspired, too, by finding their goalkeeper-captain back on top form, highlighted early on by one blinding save from point-blank range.

Chris felt, however, that he still had something to prove, to them and even to himself – that a goalie *could* lead a side successfully. He decided after the match that it was the right moment to reveal the secret plans he'd made

since that row with Luke in the mini-bus.

If ever they were to rid themselves of the haunting memories of last season, he reckoned, they'd first have to do a bit of ghost-busting!

'Well played!' he called out above the noise in the hut. 'Just listen a minute. Some people keep going on about how great Tim's team were and so it's about time we put that to the test . . .'

'Play them, you mean, like you said,' gasped Rakesh. 'I never thought you were being serious.'

'I'm deadly serious,' Chris confirmed. 'But not just play them – *beat* them! In fact, I've already gone and fixed up a challenge match.'

They were all stunned for several

seconds until Rakesh broke the silence with his usual huge cry of 'Wicked!'

Chris grinned as he saw his idea beginning to catch on with the others too. 'Tim thinks I'm crazy but he's letting Andrew skipper the Old Boys team. They're calling it *The War of the Westons*!'

'I like it!' whooped Rakesh. 'As long as your grandad's not the referee as well!'

Grandad was happy to leave that job to Mr Jones, but nothing could stop him taking up his old place on the touchline before the kick-off on Saturday morning.

It was bitterly cold, the strong autumn winds whipping through the trees on the recreation ground. But Grandad, determined to show that he was well on the way to a full recovery, intended to use his walking stick more for waving about than for leaning on. He was tightly wrapped up, however, in a heavy coat, scarf and cap, and from one of his gloved hands dangled a loose lead attached to a lively black and white collie dog.

Soon Shoot was barking out a loud welcome to the two teams as they spilled shivering from the changing hut, the red and white stripes of Dane-bridge mingling with the yellow and black kit Andrew had borrowed from Selworth school.

'Pity Bradshaw isn't playing today,' Andrew joked to Tim as they passed a practice ball between them. 'We

could all have warmed up by kicking *him* up in the air a few times!'

Tim smirked. 'Talking of fouls, just you remember which side you're on. Don't go giving a penalty away or something to help Chris out.'

'As if I would,' Andrew choked. 'He won't get any favours like that from me, don't worry.'

But when Mr Jones called the captains together, the brothers ran to the centre circle to shake hands and grinned at the strangeness of facing one another on opposing sides.

'C'mon, let's kick off quick,' hissed Andrew, shuddering. 'I'm freezing. It's OK for you with that padded goalie's jersey on.'

'I'll need it,' Chris laughed. 'I'll be

standing about most of the game having nothing to do!'

The school's green goalkeeper's top was something very special to Chris. He always felt a tingle of pride whenever he pulled it over his head and he wasn't prepared to give it up without a struggle.

He won the toss and chose to have the wind to their advantage in the second half when everyone would be tiring. 'Forget the cold,' he told his players. 'We've got to try and hold out somehow till half-time.'

As Chris took up his place in goal, he became aware of how many people had braved the bad weather to watch the match. But it was not only the crowd which made him realize how important this game was. He also

spotted somebody else skulking in the cover of the trees.

'So, Luke's here, is he?' he smiled to himself. 'I thought he might turn up, hoping to see us get thrashed. Right then, that settles it. We'll have to make sure he goes home disappointed.'

Chris knew what a setback a heavy defeat might be for him and his team, and how Luke would never let them hear the last of it. But he believed it was a risk worth taking. If they could actually pull off a victory, it might even shut Luke up for good!

Straight from the start, however, they found themselves pinned down in their own half by the strength of the wind and the Old Boys' determination to make the most of it while they could.

Time and again the ball whistled around the Danebridge goalmouth, but Andrew's men found Chris at his very best as he twisted and turned in all directions to keep them out. And when Tim did once manage to slide the ball underneath the goalie's diving body, there was Paul Walker ready on the line to hook the ball away to safety.

Chris slapped his defender on the back in relief. 'Magic, Paul! That makes up for everything.'

His new friend grinned. 'Thanks, skipper. I said I'd be right behind you from now on!'

# 6  *Bouncing Back*

Desperate for goals before half-time, the Old Boys in their yellow and black outfits buzzed around the Danebridge penalty area like swarms of angry bees. But the killing sting just would not come.

Duggie, of all people, was guilty of the worst miss. Finding the ball at his feet smack in front of goal, he crashed his shot up against the crossbar. He struck it so hard, the bar was still twanging several seconds after the ball had rebounded out of play.

Andrew spurred his team forward with shaking fists and frantic arm waving, unable to understand how they had so far failed to score. If possible, he intended to put that right himself.

The next time he received the ball, he was just outside the area and looked up to see Duggie and Tim both moving in for a centre. But he also saw Chris standing off his line, ready to cut out the expected cross. Instead, Andrew tried a lob over his brother's head.

'Goal!' he screamed, but then watched in horror as the wind caught hold of the ball and stopped it floating out of reach. Chris was able to leap, stretch back and claw the ball down to one side for a corner.

'No! Save of the season, you mean!' laughed Rakesh.

But Chris didn't want any fuss, despite all the applause from the spectators around the pitch. There was work to be done. 'C'mon, concentrate,' he bellowed. 'Mark their men.'

Too late. Duggie beat Paul to Tim's pinpoint corner, only to see his header flash straight into Chris's grateful arms.

'We're never going to score today,' Duggie groaned. 'He must have a ball magnet stuffed up that green jersey of his.'

The Old Boys kept up the pressure right until half-time but when Mr Jones blew the whistle, the score was still 0–0. They slumped together on the ground in disbelief while, nearby, their younger opponents were noisily jubilant. Not even the headmaster's warning that the match was far from over was enough to calm the Danebridge lads down.

'We've got the wind in our favour now,' Chris grinned. 'Let's go out and give *them* something to worry about at last.'

He should have known better. As Chris gave Grandad a thumbs-up sign at the start of the second half, he was forgetting that nobody could ever afford to relax against any side led by his older brother.

Andrew didn't know the meaning of giving up. He drove his players on again into the teeth of a wind which had increased almost to gale force. Winning the ball himself in midfield,

he knocked it to Tim who slipped a pass with swift, deadly accuracy into Duggie's stride.

The striker shot quickly on the run before Chris could smother the chance, although the goalkeeper still managed to get a hand to the ball. He deflected it slightly but, sadly for Danebridge, not quite enough.

The ball clipped the inside of one post, bounced along the line to glance against the other and then plopped gently over into the goal.

Duggie held up his arms in triumph. '1–0!' he yelled before being swamped by his celebrating teammates.

'We've got 'em! The floodgates will open now,' Andrew forecast confidently. 'This is gonna be a massacre!'

Chris feared the worst too, but even

the older lads found it very difficult playing into such a powerful wind. Any ball that was lofted into the air simply blew back over their heads and Danebridge were able gradually to press them further and further back on the defensive.

Simon Garner, Chris's old rival for the number one jersey, became by far the busier of the two goalkeepers. Each time the ball was blown out of play he had to run and fetch it, and then belt it for all he was worth just to get the goal kick beyond his own penalty area.

From one of these, however, the ball fell fatally to the feet of Rakesh, carelessly left unmarked. The winger accepted the free gift with glee before

lashing it straight back past Simon's despairing dive.

'The equalizer!' screamed Rakesh. 'We've done it!'

Even Grandad was seen celebrating, waving his stick so much that it set Shoot off barking in alarm. 'Sorry, m'boy,' he chuckled, feeling foolish. 'Mustn't get over-excited. Doctor's orders, you know.'

Mr Jones checked his watch to see there were just five minutes left. Briefly, he wondered whether to finish the game early with honours even at 1–1, but let play go on. Although all the boys were weary, both teams were still battling away fiercely for the winner.

First it nearly went to the Old Boys. Duggie broke clear of the Danebridge defence but, thinking he was offside, hesitated and allowed Chris time to race out of goal and snatch the ball off his toes.

Then it was Chris's turn to launch his side on yet another attack. Finding himself on the edge of his area, he decided to use the great strength of the wind to send the ball way down-field for Rakesh to chase.

Taking a big breath, he leathered the ball with all the muscle power his leg could muster. His boot connected like the bang from a cannon and the cannonball itself was blasted high into the air.

'Wow!' Chris gasped aloud. 'I really got hold of that one.'

Carried by the gale, the ball covered an enormous distance before starting

to drop to earth deep into the Old Boys' territory, making Andrew back-pedal furiously to try and deal with it. Most of the defenders were glad to leave it to their skipper, but Simon panicked and charged madly out of his goal to lay claim to it as well.

Both players were also keeping an eye on Rakesh, who was rapidly closing in from the left, and in the swirling wind none of them could really judge just where the ball would come down.

'Watch the bounce!' Tim shrieked as it finally hit the ground not far in front of them, but his warning was in vain.

By the time Andrew and Simon realized the danger themselves, they had collided with one another and toppled over in an untidy, tangled heap. Untouched, the football leapt up high again like a runaway horse and

not even the nippy Rakesh could catch it.

There was no net on the goal to halt its progress either. After two more bounces Chris's monster kick sailed between the posts to the open-mouthed astonishment of all the players, not least Chris himself.

His own teammates were the first to recover from the shock and they ran back to mob their captain in delight. A dazed Andrew meanwhile could only appeal to Mr Jones. 'Is that allowed? Can a goalie score?'

'Certainly,' the headmaster confirmed. 'It is rare, but there's no rule against it.'

Andrew shook his head as if to clear it of a bad dream, but this was more terrible than his worst nightmare. Not

only were his team losing, it looked like his kid brother had gone and scored the winning goal!

And so it proved. When Mr Jones blew for full-time, however, he was pleased to see how well the older lads took their unexpected 2–1 defeat. To Andrew's great credit, he hid his deep disappointment behind an embarrassed grin and even beat Chris in calling for 'Three Cheers'.

But after Chris had led the response, Andrew grabbed him. 'Just wait till I get you home,' he cried, and then laughed as Chris looked suddenly worried. 'Only joking. Well done, our kid. That big kick of yours was incredible!'

Chris beamed. 'It was a get-well-soon present for Grandad.'

They glanced across to the touchline to see Grandad dancing around with Shoot and letting the dog jump up all over him.

'It seems to have worked anyway,' Andrew giggled. 'So I guess I'll have to let you off this time.'

Mr Jones also had Grandad in mind. 'I expect you'll be glad to get back inside for a nice hot cup of tea, won't you?' he called out.

'Aye,' Grandad replied, 'but it's done my old heart a world of good to see the lads play such a grand match. A real tonic!'

The headmaster nodded. 'After a captain's performance like that from young Chris, the school team should go from strength to strength.'

'Just like me,' smiled Grandad.

'Reckon I won't be needing this any longer.'

He bent down and offered his walking stick to Shoot. 'Here, boy, take it,' he said, and the dog immediately grabbed it between his jaws, hardly seeming to believe his luck.

'He can carry the stick home for me,' Grandad chuckled. 'As Chris has found out, there comes a time when we've all got to stand on our own two feet!'

**THE END**